Goldilocks and the Three Bears

Written by
Tony Mitton

Illustrated by
Liz Million

WALKER BOOKS
AND SUBSIDIARIES
LONDON • BOSTON • SYDNEY • AUCKLAND

One day
as Goldilocks explores,
she snoops around
and sees ...

By the fire
she finds
three chairs
and one of them
just fits,
but when she
settles down in it...

Too high!

Three bears
come home hungrily
but one
begins to whine,
"We left our porridge
here to cool ...

Mum and Dad do all they can to comfort Baby Bear, but just then Baby points and shrieks...

Hey!

For Margaret, Michael, Imogen
and Fraser, from all the Mitton-McKellars
T.M.

Lots of love and thanks to my lovely relatives,
Mum, Dad, Rach, Paul, Nana, Gramps, and Nana Millie
L.M.

First published 2000 by Walker Books Ltd
87 Vauxhall Walk, London SE11 5HJ

This edition published 2008

2 4 6 8 10 9 7 5 3 1

Text © 2000 Tony Mitton

Illustrations © 2000 Liz Million

The moral rights of the author and illustrator have been asserted.

Printed in China

British Library Cataloguing in Publication Data:
a catalogue record for this book is available from the British Library.

ISBN 978-1-4063-1673-5

www.walkerbooks.co.uk